U0022234

For Gemk,

Whose endless supply of ideas and honest critique made this possible.

感謝 Gemk

源源不絕的靈感及誠懇的建議讓這一切成真。

The Ugly Ducklings

新醜小鴨

Coleen Reddy 著

陳澤新 繪

薛慧儀 譯

ㄇㄇ 三民書局

Mother Duck was sitting on her batch of eggs.
She was waiting for her little ducks to hatch.
Under her, the eggs were warm and cozy.

鴨媽媽坐在一窩鴨蛋上，
等著她的小鴨鴨孵化出來。
在她肚子底下的鴨蛋們，個個是溫暖又舒適。

Soon, she heard a noise.

"It's happening!" she thought excitedly.

The eggs started hatching.

不久，她聽到一陣小小的噪音。
「鴨寶寶要出生了！」她興奮地想著。
蛋開始孵化囉！

One by one, little heads started peering out of their eggs.
Mother Duck cleaned and fed them.
Only one egg hadn't hatched.

鴨寶寶的頭一個接一個地，慢慢從蛋殼裡探了出來。
鴨媽媽把鴨寶寶們清理乾淨，並且餵他們吃東西。
只有一顆蛋還沒有孵出來。

7

Two days had gone by and still the last egg hadn't hatched.

"It's very unusual," thought Mother Duck.

Just as she was about to get Dr. Duck, the egg hatched.

兩天過去了，最後一顆蛋還是沒有動靜。
「這實在太奇怪了！」鴨媽媽想。
就在她想要去叫鴨醫生來的時候，這顆蛋破殼了！

Out popped a...well...a something. But it certainly was NOT a duck.
"What's this?" thought Mother Duck. "I don't understand."
It was a strange little thing. It was bigger than the other ducklings.
It had an unusual red crest on its head.

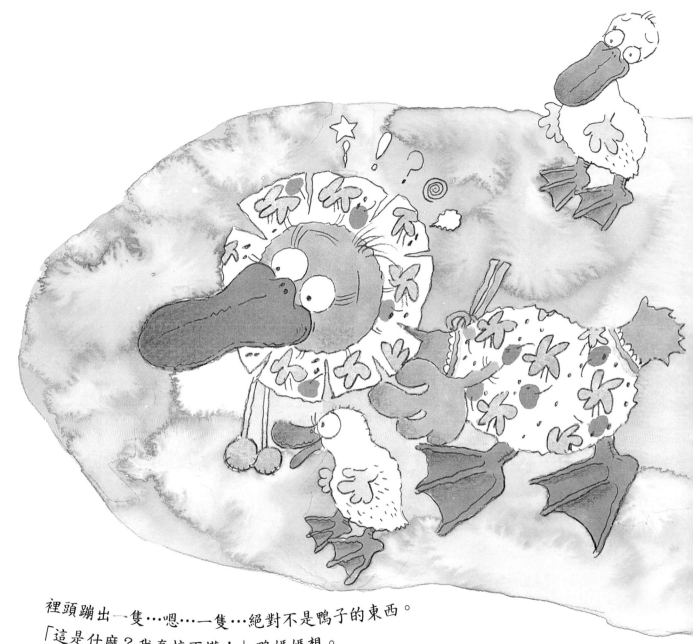

裡頭蹦出一隻…嗯…一隻…絕對不是鴨子的東西。

「這是什麼？我真搞不懂！」鴨媽媽想。

那是一隻很奇怪的小東西，長得比其他的鴨寶寶都來得大，

而且頭上還有一個不尋常的紅色鳥冠！

11

The little thing was very quiet.
It lay down and didn't want to do anything that
the other ducklings did.
It watched everything they did, but it refused to join in.

這小東西很安靜。

他總是乖乖地趴著，一點都不想做其他鴨寶寶在做的事情。

他看著鴨寶寶們的一舉一動，卻不願加入他們的行列。

Some days later, it suddenly got up.

"Look here," it said to the ducklings.

"I'm not like you. I'm very different. I think I know why.

You're just ordinary ducklings. I'm not.

I'm a king of some sort. I'm royalty!

This crest on my head here is a crown. I'm UNIQUE!"

幾天後，他突然站了起來。
「看我這裡，」他對鴨寶寶們說，
「我一點都不像你們，我是很不一樣的。我知道為什麼。
因為你們只是普通的鴨寶寶，但我不是，
我是個天生的鳥王，我有貴族血統！
我頭上的鳥冠就是王冠。我是獨一無二的！」

"Are you sure that you're a king?" asked Mother Duck.

"Of course," said the king. "That means that you are my servants.

You must do whatever I say. Bring me my food and keep me happy.

Don't worry, I'll teach you how to treat royalty.

First, you must learn how to bow,

and you must call me 'Your Majesty' and...."

「你確定自己真的是鳥王嗎？」鴨媽媽問。

「當然囉！」鳥王說。「這表示你們都是我的僕人！
你們必須要服從我的命令，提供食物給我，還要讓我心情愉快。
別擔心，我會教你們如何侍奉皇族的。
首先，你們一定要學習如何彎腰鞠躬，
而且要叫我『陛下』，還有……」

What an odd picture they made!
The king sat on a little rock and all the little ducklings bowed
and took his orders. But he was not a good king.
If anything did not please him, he would yell,
"You ugly ducklings! You can't do anything right."
The king thought he was very handsome
and the ducklings were very ugly!
He was very unfriendly to them.

多麼奇怪的畫面呀！
鳥王坐在一塊小石頭上，鴨寶寶們對他彎腰鞠躬，
聽候他的吩咐。但他可不是個好國王，
如果惹得他不高興的話，他就會大喊：
「你們這些醜小鴨！什麼都做不好！」
鳥王覺得自己英俊的不得了，
而這些鴨寶寶簡直是醜死了！
他對鴨寶寶們非常地不友善。

The king would send the ducklings to far-off places to get the special
worms that he liked to eat. The ducklings grew quite unhappy.
On one of these trips, the ducklings found themselves at a farm.
They were curious to see what the farm animals and birds looked like.

鳥王會叫鴨寶寶們到很遠的地方，去抓一種他喜歡吃的蟲。
鴨寶寶們越來越不高興了。
有一次，在幫鳥王找蟲的途中，鴨寶寶們來到一座農場。
他們好奇地想知道，農場裡的動物和鳥長得是什麼模樣。

They gasped when they saw a whole lot of birds that
looked exactly like their king.
They immediately started bowing and calling them, "Your Majesties."
"What are you doing?" asked one of the kings.

當他們看到一大群和他們的鳥王長得一模一樣的鳥時，
都嚇得屏住了呼吸。
他們馬上對這些鳥彎腰鞠躬，還叫他們「陛下」。
「你們在做什麼呀？」其中一隻鳥王問。

23

But the ducklings were so scared that they ran away.
They came back to their king and told him about what they had seen.
"If there are other kings like myself, then I must fight them,"
said the king. "Maybe they want to take over my kingdom.
Tomorrow, we must go to war!"

但是鴨寶寶們實在太害怕了，馬上轉頭就跑。

他們跑回自己的鳥王面前，告訴他剛才他們看見了什麼。

「如果有其他像我這樣的鳥王，那我就必須和他們戰鬥！」鳥王說。

「說不定他們想奪走我的王國呢！明天，我們就要向他們宣戰！」

The next day, they set out for the farm.
The king was wearing his splendid robes,
and he had his crown adorned with a garland.
The ducklings carried him, because royalty
didn't actually walk through mud.
The ducklings were afraid of fighting,
but they were more afraid of their king.

第二天，他們便往農場出發了。
鳥王穿上他閃亮的長袍，還在王冠上戴了花圈。
鴨寶寶們抬著他前進，因為貴族是不在爛泥地上走的。
鴨寶寶們都害怕打仗，但是他們卻更害怕他們的鳥王！

They entered the farm.

The frightened ducklings gently lowered the king onto the ground while all the birds watched with surprised looks.

"I have come to conquer your kingdom," said the king.

"Do you surrender or not?"

他們進入了農莊。

嚇壞的鴨寶寶們輕輕地把鳥王
放到地上，其他的鳥兒驚訝地
看著他們。

「我來征服你們的王國！」鳥王說。「你們要不要投降？」

The other birds seemed confused. They said nothing.

"Charge!" yelled the king.

The ducklings just stood there.

"You ugly ducklings!" yelled the king. "You're useless."

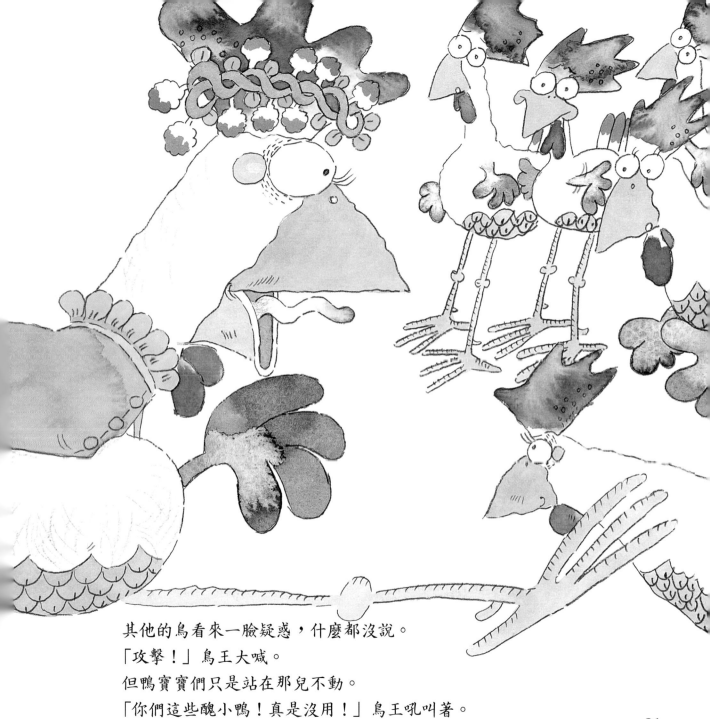

其他的鳥看來一臉疑惑，什麼都沒說。
「攻擊！」鳥王大喊。
但鴨寶寶們只是站在那兒不動。
「你們這些醜小鴨！真是沒用！」鳥王吼叫著。

One of the farm birds stepped forward and said,
"Don't listen to him, little ducklings.
He is not a king and you are not his servants.
This bird is a rooster just like us."
The roosters pulled off the king's garland and robes.

有隻農場的鳥兒站出來說：「小鴨子們，別聽他的！他不是鳥王，
你們也不是他的僕人。這隻鳥和我們一樣，只是一隻公雞而已。」
公雞們把鳥王的花圈和長袍扯了下來。

"The stork must have made a mistake with you. She is getting very old now. Last week she delivered a vulture instead of a rooster."

"That's not true," yelled the king. "I was born with this crown."

The roosters at the farm started laughing. "That's not a crown; that's a comb. We all have those combs on our heads."

「鸛鳥一定是把你送錯地方了。她真是年紀大了，
　上星期她還把兀鷹當成公雞送過來呢！」
「胡說！」鳥王喊著。「我天生就有這頂王冠的！」
　　　農場裡的公雞都笑了起來。「那才不是王冠，那是雞冠！
　　我們頭上也都有雞冠呀。」

The ducklings started turning away.

"Come back," yelled the king. But it was no good.

The ducklings had deserted him.

The old "king" was left with the other roosters on the farm.

His days of being a king were over.

鴨寶寶們開始一個個轉身離開。

「回來！回來！」鳥王喊著，但一點用也沒有，

鴨寶寶們已經不理他了。於是這隻「鳥王」被留在

農場裡和其他公雞一起待著。

他當鳥王的日子已經結束了。

37

But it is said, that until he was an old grandfather with many grandchildren, he continued to bore everyone with his tales of being a king.

The ducklings grew up to be beautiful ducks.

They told their grandchildren about a crazy, ugly bird that thought he was a king.

但是，據說一直到他成了老爺爺，有了很多
孫子後，他還是不停地講著他當鳥王的故事，
大家都聽煩了。
鴨寶寶們也長大了，個個都變成了漂亮的鴨子。
他們也講故事給鴨孫子們聽：「以前啊，有隻又瘋又醜的鳥，
一直以為他自己是個鳥王呢！」

用松果，做公雞

工具與材料

1. 松果
2. 色紙或羽毛
3. 西卡紙
4. 彩紋紙
5. 雙面膠
6. 剪刀
7. 塑膠眼睛
8. 黏土
9. 牙籤

＊在做勞作之前，要記得在桌上先鋪一張紙或墊板，
　才不會把桌面弄得髒兮兮喔！

步　驟

1. 將色紙剪成羽毛的形狀，做好之後，將羽毛（或原本就準備好的羽毛）用雙面膠
　固定在松果的後端。
2. 再用黏土揉一個圓形，做為公雞的頭部，在上面黏上塑膠眼睛、雞冠和雞嘴。
3. 將做好的雞頭固定在牙籤上，再用西卡紙圍著牙籤做雞的脖子。
4. 用彩紋紙裝飾雞脖子。
5. 將雞脖子及雞的頭固定在松果的前端。

生字表

　p. 2

batch [bætʃ] 名 一批

hatch [hætʃ] 動 孵化

cozy [`kozɪ] 形 舒適的

　p. 6

peer [pɪr] 動 出現，露出

feed [fid] 動 餵食

　p. 8

unusual [ʌn`juʒʊəl] 形 不尋常的

　*p. 10*

pop [pɑp] 動 突然砰出

crest [krɛst] 名 鳥冠

　*p. 14*

ordinary [`ɔrdə,nɛrɪ] 形 普通的，
　　正常的

royalty [`rɔɪəltɪ] 名 王室，皇族

crown [kraun] 名 王冠

　*p. 16*

Your Majesty 陛下

　*p. 18*

odd [ɑd] 形 奇怪的；古怪的

yell [jɛl] 動 大聲喊叫

　*p. 20*

worm [wɝm] 名 蟲

　*p. 22*

gasp [gæsp] 動 嚇得屏息

immediately [ɪ`midɪɪtlɪ] 副 立刻，
　　馬上

41

全新創作 **英文讀本**
帶給你優格（yogurt）般，青春的酸甜滋味！

附中英雙語CD
（共八冊）
適讀年齡：10歲以上

Teens' Chronicles

愛閱雙語叢書

青春記事簿

大維的驚奇派對／秀寶貝，說故事／杰生的大秘密
傑克的戀愛初體驗／誰是他爸爸？
叛逆大維打工記／外星老師來上課／耶！放假了！

你我身上純真的影子，
透過一篇篇幽默風趣的故事重現，
推薦你這套青春無悔的創作系列，
讓愛玫、杰生、大維、凱爾、海倫、傑克，
帶你進入他們的世界，品味另一種學習英語的全新感受。

中高級・中英對照

探索英文叢書

波波唸翻天系列

你知道可愛的小兔子也會 "碎碎唸" 嗎？
波波就是這樣。
他將要告訴我們什麼有趣的故事呢？

波波的復活節／波波的西部冒險記／波波上課記／我愛你，波波
波波的下雪天／波波郊遊去／波波打球記／聖誕快樂，波波／波波的萬聖夜

共 9 本，每本均附 CD

國家圖書館出版品預行編目資料

The Ugly Ducklings:新醜小鴨 / Coleen Reddy著;
陳澤新繪;薛慧儀譯.－－初版一刷.－－臺北
市;三民,2003
　　面; 公分－－(愛閱雙語叢書.二十六個妙朋
友系列) 中英對照
　ISBN 957-14-3758-1　(精裝)

　1.英國語言－讀本

523.38　　　　　　　　　　　　　　92008821

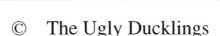

© **The Ugly Ducklings**
—— 新醜小鴨

著作人	Coleen Reddy
繪　圖	陳澤新
譯　者	薛慧儀
發行人	劉振強
著作財產權人	三民書局股份有限公司 臺北市復興北路386號
發行所	三民書局股份有限公司 地址／臺北市復興北路386號 電話／(02)25006600 郵撥／0009998-5
印刷所	三民書局股份有限公司
門市部	復北店／臺北市復興北路386號 重南店／臺北市重慶南路一段61號
初版一刷	2003年7月
編　號	S 85654-1
定　價	新臺幣壹佰捌拾元整

行政院新聞局登記證局版臺業字第○二○○號

有著作權・不准侵害

ISBN　957-14-3758-1　　(精裝)